W9-BTL-694

POWER
FORWARD

Also by Hena Khan

Amina's Voice

It's Ramadan, Curious George

Golden Domes and Silver Lanterns:
A Muslim Book of Colors

Night of the Moon: A Muslim Holiday Story

More in the Zayd Saleem, Chasing the Dream series

On Point

Bounce Back (Coming soon!)

BOOK 1

HENA KHAN

ILLUSTRATED BY
SALLY WERN COMPORT

SALAAM
READS
NEW YORK | LONDON | TORONTO
SYDNEY | NEW DELHI

An imprint of Simon & Schuster Children's Publishing Division
1230 Avenue of the Americas, New York, New York 10020

Also available in a SALAAM READS hardcover edition
Book design by Dan Potash
The text for this book was set in Iowan Old Style.
The illustrations for this book were rendered in Prismacolor pencil on Denril and digital.
Manufactured in the United States of America
0820 OFF
First SALAAM READS paperback edition May 2018
10 9 8 7 6
Library of Congress Cataloging-in-Publication Data
Names: Khan, Hena, author.
Title: Power forward / Hena Khan.
Description: First edition. | New York : Salaam Reads, [2018] | Series: Zayd Saleem, chasing the dream | Summary: Fourth-grader Zayd yearns to play basketball on the Gold Team, but when he skips orchestra rehearsal to practice, his parents forbid anything basketball-related, and tryouts are coming soon.
Identifiers: LCCN 2017036293 (print) | LCCN 2017047750 (eBook)
ISBN 9781534411982 (hc) | ISBN 9781534411999 (pbk) | ISBN 9781534412002 (eBook)
Subjects: | CYAC: Basketball—Fiction. | Pakistani Americans—Fiction. | Family life—Fiction. | Honesty—Fiction. | Middle schools—Fiction. | Schools—Fiction.
Classification: LCC PZ7.K52652 (eBook) | LCC PZ7.K52652 Pow 2018 (print) | DDC [Fic]—dc23
LC record available at https://lccn.loc.gov/2017036293

you for cheering me on throughout life, and for inspiring characters that might resemble you at times. And finally, my incredible teammates: my husband, Farrukh, and sons, Bilal and Humza, not only lived many of the experiences in this series but also helped me to weave them into a story with humor and heart—and the right basketball terminology.

You will forever be my MVPs.

ACKNOWLEDGMENTS

Writing this series, which was like winning a championship game to me, was only possible because of the wonderful team that helped it come to life. My super-smart and insightful agent, Matthew Elblonk, signed me with the awesome Salaam Reads team. Coach Zareen Jaffery shared my passion for the series and used her expert editing skills to bring out the best in these books, along with the vision of Dan Potash and the design group at Simon & Schuster. I'm lucky to work out with talented trainers, including Ann McCallum, Joan Waites, Laura Gehl, Afgen Sheikh, and Andrea Menotti, who pushed me to exercise my writing muscles and offered invaluable advice. I also have the best fans in the world: my beloved parents, siblings, and friends. Thank

For Farrukh

1

I've imagined lots of ways to get famous. The best of all would be if I took a game-winning shot in the NBA finals. But I wouldn't mind being a magician who slices people in half on *America's Got Talent*. I'd like to set the Guinness World Record for burping the Chinese alphabet. I've seen lots of YouTube videos. I know what it takes to become famous.

I never, ever, imagined getting famous by playing the violin at the Brisk River Elementary School fall concert.

The concert program booklet calls it a "memorable night of musical escape." The sweaty audience slumped on rows of metal folding chairs looks ready to escape. It feels like three hundred degrees in the school cafeteria. But "memorable"? I'm sure everyone will forget tonight as soon as they rush out the doors to the parking lot.

Ms. Sterling is waving her baton like she's conducting the National Symphony Orchestra, not the fourth-grade orchestra. I'm sitting on the second level of the stage, melting in a white shirt, black pants, and purple clip-on bow tie. It's extra hot because I'm wearing my basketball

training jersey and shorts underneath. I ran over from the gym right after practice. And I couldn't find my dress shoes this morning, so I'm in my sneakers. My basketball and empty water bottle are tucked under my chair.

Our third song goes perfectly. Ms. Sterling raises her hands, soaking in the applause. Next is our finale, "Tribal Lament." It ends with a cool drum solo by Antonio. I raise my violin to my chin. Abigail, who's sitting next to me, starts to whisper.

"Zayd! I need more room." She sticks her bow out so far that it almost touches my face.

"See?" she whines. "Move over!"

I scoot my chair to the right a few inches and start playing.

"I need more room!" Abigail hisses.

It looks like Abigail has plenty of room, but she's glaring at me. So I scoot over again, way over to the edge of the riser. I shift in my seat, still playing, and then—oh no! My chair tips over and I'm falling. AHHHHH!

I see my life flashing before my eyes. Wait, no. Phew. It's the flashes of everyone's cameras. And then, CRASH! I land smack in the middle of the drums, barely missing Antonio. My chair clangs to the floor somewhere behind me. WHACK! My basketball smacks me on the head before bouncing into the audience.

All the music stops. I hear gasps from the crowd. Then there's nothing but silence. Ms. Sterling rushes over to me, her face pale.

"Zayd! Are you okay? Can you move?" she shrieks.

I nod, take her hand, and slowly stand up. My shirt is untucked and a little torn, and my bright red training jersey is peeking through. My bow tie is missing. But nothing seems broken, especially not my playing arms. For playing *basketball,* I mean. I can't afford to be injured. My league has tryouts coming up in just four weeks, and I have to make the gold team.

Ms. Sterling looks like she's about to cry. I can feel everyone's eyes fixed on me. And then, suddenly, I understand what "the show must go on" means.

I face the audience and take an extra-deep bow. Everyone cheers, whistles, and applauds. And then I actually get . . . a STANDING OVATION! I bow again and can't help but laugh with the crowd. I rub my head where the basketball hit me, and someone from the audience throws it back to me.

As I climb back onto the risers, Abigail helps me set up my chair.

"Sorry," she mumbles.

If you had told me I was going to be famous today, I wouldn't have believed it. My older sister Zara posted a video of my fall on YouTube. It's already been viewed forty thousand times. In six hours! I can only imagine how famous I'll be by tomorrow. And in the end, this concert might actually be memorable after all.

2

Today I'm on fire. Not on fire as in "stop, drop, and roll." On fire as in *completely unstoppable* on the basketball court.

It's almost the end of practice, and I've got a steal, six baskets, and four rebounds. All the soreness I felt the day after I fell off the stage is gone. Right now I feel amazing. This is my best scrimmage of the season.

"Stop standing!" Coach shouts. Alex and his headband dribble past four of us to score an easy layup.

I inbound the ball and run down the court. Sweat is dripping onto my face. Alex looks cool in a headband, but Zara says they make me look like a dork. So I wipe the sweat onto my sleeve.

I yank up my shorts as I run. My mom had to sew in a tighter elastic, like with most of my shorts, since the drawstring doesn't pull. I don't understand why they make gym shorts with fake strings that hang there, like lost shoelaces that don't actually *do* anything.

Chris throws me the ball past half-court, and I dribble with my left hand. I cross over to my right to get by a defender. Then I pass it to

Keanu and . . . SWISH! He hits an easy shot from right outside the paint.

Coach is nodding now, and he mutters, "All right, all right." That's like hearing "good job" from someone who actually praises kids. Not Coach. He groans extra loud, clamps his hands over his head, and screams at us from the sideline. Mama says he must sweat out five pounds during our games. But I get it.

Coach Wheeler lives for basketball, like me. Plus, he makes us work hard. In my old league we had a super-nice coach. But all we got was a sportsmanship award after losing every game by twenty points or more. This season I'm playing better. And we've been winning, too.

"Nice pass," Keanu says to me after Coach blows the whistle.

Coach blows the whistle again, and I

inbound the ball. William dribbles down to the three-point line and passes to Chris. I pause, and my brain goes into overdrive. It's like I'm seeing everything in slow motion. I've been hot today. What better way to end the scrimmage, and impress Coach, than by taking a winning shot?

I glance over at Keanu, and then, instead of setting a screen, call for the ball. Chris passes it to me. I'm

feeling confident as I dribble, pump fake, and launch a shot that goes straight into the hoop.

SIZZLE.

Did I mention I'm on fire?

Coach kind of half smiles at me when I pass him to grab my water bottle from the bench. My heart beats quicker as I imagine playing this well during tryouts. If I do, I have a real chance at moving up from the D league to the gold team.

My best friend Adam is on the gold team, and it's my dream for the two of us to play together. Plus I hate the way D league sounds. I know the *D* stands for "developmental," but it's always felt like a bad grade or something. I'm ready to go for the gold.

3

My dad says that good things come always in threes. Number 1: I had an awesome practice. Number 2: I spot my grandmother's car with a giant gold-and-green "ALLAH" medallion hanging from the rearview mirror. It pulls up in the pickup lane. I can't wait to see what number three will be.

Naano isn't like grandmothers you see on TV. She doesn't smother me with hugs, bake me cookies, or say things like "bless your heart." She won't let me shake her hand until I wash mine first. The only cookies in her house come in crinkly packages. And her favorite sayings are curses in Urdu. In other words, she's awesome.

"Mama's still in meeting. You win?" she asks as I crawl into the back seat. The car smells like cardamom and muscle rub.

"Yeah, but it was just practice," I say. "Not a real game."

"Humph. Win next game. You will."

It's a statement. Like she knows the future. Naano kind of speaks like Yoda.

We get to her house, and my grandfather, Nana Abu, is napping. That means Naano can focus on feeding me. The only thing she's more obsessed with than the perfect cup of chai is how to fatten up "skinny mouse." That's her nickname for me.

"Paratha?" she asks. Before I open my mouth, she uncovers a bowl draped with a towel and pulls off a chunk of dough. Even though she shuffles when she walks, her hands move with lightning speed. I wish I could dribble as fast as she rolls out the dough into a perfect flat circle. She slices butter into it, folds it up, rolls it out again, and puts it on a pan. I watch it sizzle and bubble up, and realize I'm starving.

"Sugar?" Naano doesn't wait for an answer again. The paratha is resting on a plate. She smears more butter on top, sprinkles it with sugar, and hands it to me.

I devour it while Naano watches me with

a satisfied smile on her face. This was nothing like the baked veggie chips and healthy granola bars that Mama's been giving me for snacks lately.

"Milk? You need milk," she says. She starts to get up to go to the fridge.

"No thanks, Naano, I don't like milk." As I say the words, Naano slumps back in her chair. It's like I've personally insulted her. But my stomach hurts when I drink milk. Or maybe I just don't like it. I'm not sure.

My mom wants me to keep track of the things I eat and what makes my stomach hurt. She said that way we can figure out if something is wrong with me, like an allergy or something. That's when Zara said, "There's definitely something wrong with you," and I pushed her, and Mama yelled at us both for fighting.

A few days later Mama gave me a notebook called FOOD JOURNAL and wrote on half the pages:

DATE/TIME:

WHAT I ATE:

HOW I FEEL:

I thought she was kidding, but she wasn't. Writing in the journal feels like homework, and I always forget to do it. Plus nobody else I know has to do anything like this.

"Oh, my dramas!" Snack time is over. Naano shuffles to the family room and shakes and mutters at the remote until the TV is on, extra loud.

I used to be able go outside and practice free throws on the old hoop that belonged to my uncle, Jamal Mamoo. But last month my grandfather backed his car into it and it fell over. I pull out a book and pretend to be more interested in it than in Naano's show, *Dil Nahi Chahta*. I watch it every couple of weeks or so when I'm visiting. But the story changes so slowly I can follow along, even though I only speak a few words of Urdu. What I've figured out is:

- ✓ The main character wants to make movies and is always running around with a big camera trying to film people who slam doors in his face.
- ✓ His parents are really mad at him because they want him to be a doctor and marry their best friends' daughter.
- ✓ The camera randomly cuts from one frozen angry face to another around the room while intense music plays.
- ✓ Every three minutes or so there's a commercial break. Most commercials are for cheap flights to India, frozen Indian foods, and some guy named Prem Jyotish who REALLY wants you to call him today.

When I start to laugh because the guy follows an old lady into a fabric store with his camera, and she slams the door in his face, Naano shushes me.

"Where is your mother? Isn't it time for you to go home?" She says it like it could be a joke, but I can't tell for sure.

Naano waits for the next commercial and goes into the kitchen to make chai. And then the doorbell rings.

My mom bursts inside, scanning the room like she's lost something until she sees me. She gives me a tired smile.

"Asalaamualaikum. How was practice, sweetie?" she says. "Sorry. I didn't expect to be so late."

"You want chai? Paratha?" Naano calls out from the kitchen.

"I'm good." Mama turns to Naano. "You

really should watch your diet, Ammi, and stop making parathas. That's a lot of carbs."

"Bakwas," snorts Naano. That's her favorite word. I think it means something like "nonsense," and she says it all the time. "I'll show you carbs."

"Thanks for picking Zayd up." Mama gives Naano a hug. "See you this weekend."

"Next time I make my skinny mouse aloo paratha," Naano says to me with a wink.

Mama shakes her head. Those are parathas stuffed with potatoes. But I can't wait. Good things *do* come in threes, and that paratha was number three.

4

We pull up into the driveway, and who's there, taking free throws? Zara. Ugh. It's not fair. My sister doesn't love basketball like me, but she's amazing at it. She's good at everything she does. And she's done everything, from tae kwon do to gymnastics to basket weaving.

"What's up?" Zara tosses me the ball as I get out of the car. I take a shot, and it hits the rim hard and bounces into the neighbor's yard. In my defense, the rim is a little bent.

"Nothing," I say. I chase after the ball and fling it sideways toward the hoop again. But it smacks the side of the backboard. Then it almost hits me in the face, like a boomerang.

"Nice," Zara says as she grabs and swishes the ball through the net. It's like Zara sucked up all of my good energy from earlier.

"I'm going inside," I say. I grab my stuff from Mama's car and drag it into the house. Maybe Zara isn't trying to show off, but it's still annoying. I know I'm better at basketball than Zara, and better than the D league. I just need to prove it during tryouts.

"Asalaamualaikum, Baba." My father is

back from an overnight trip and is taking off his shoes. He gives me a hug.

"Walaikum asalaam. How was school yesterday?"

"Fine." I can't even remember what happened at school. It feels like ages ago.

"Did you have your math test?"

"Yeah."

Baba keeps looking at me with his eyebrows raised. He wants more detail.

"I did okay, I think. We didn't get it back yet. But, Baba, can we get a new hoop?"

"A what?"

I take a deep breath.

"Our rim's bent, and my shots don't go in. And the height thingy is rusted. Can we get a new basketball hoop? A good one, like Adam's? I need to practice for tryouts."

Baba sighs.

"I just got home. Can we talk about this later?"

"Okay." He didn't say no. I can work with that.

I kick off my shoes and head to my room. There's a framed photo over my bed of John Wall making a behind-the-back pass that Adam got me for my birthday. On my other wall I tacked up a poster of Michael Jordan flying through the air for a slam dunk. Even my comforter that Mama found at a bargain bedding shop has a basketball pattern on it. The threads started coming out after only a few weeks, but I still love it.

If it were up to my mom, my room would look completely different. She suggested a musical theme, with musical-note decals on the walls and violin-decorated bedding.

"How about I make printouts of all your favorite composers?" she said. I'm not even kidding. She thought I'd rather look at a bunch of old guys in powdered wigs than basketball legends.

"Zayd! Dinner!" Mama calls.

"What's this?" Zara wrinkles her nose as we sit around the table.

"Spinach cakes."

"It's so . . . *green*." Zara pokes her spinach cake with her fork. "Spinach" and "cake" are two words that should never be put together. Like "fart" and "marshmallow." It doesn't sound right.

"Green means filled with vitamins. We need to eat healthier. Try it."

I think about this afternoon's paratha and sigh.

"Zayd, don't forget to practice violin after you shower," Mama says. She scoops salad onto my plate.

"Do we have creamy dressing?" Baba asks. He's also eying his food with suspicion. I imagine the three of us look like a scene from Naano's show, *Dil Nahi Chahta*. The camera would cut to each of our eyes, staring at our plates in fear.

"That's filled with fat and chemicals. Try this olive oil and vinegar," Mama says.

Meals like this are why my grandmother and mother disagree about me. Naano says my mother feeds me "grass," and that's the reason I'm so skinny. She likes to serve me lots of red meat, fried foods, and sugar. When we go to the grocery store together, Naano even buys me cheddar-jalapeño Cheetos.

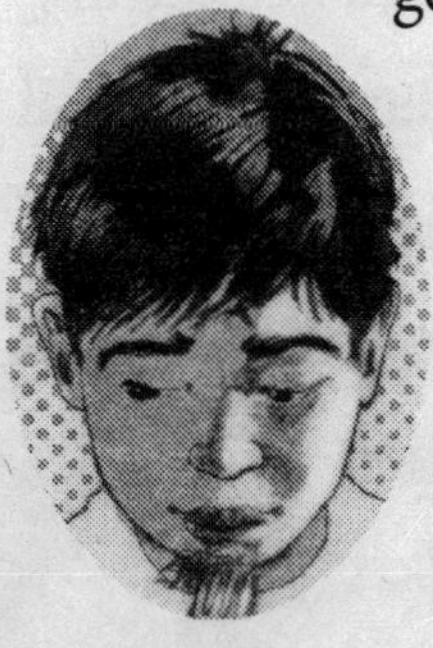

Ever since my mom watched some movie about a guy who ate nothing but McDonald's for a month and made himself sick, she decided we all need to eat less junk food. And she acts like Naano is trying to poison me. But if I had to choose which food to be scared of, I'd pick this bright green spinach cake. Cheetos may have seventeen ingredients I can't pronounce. But they look perfect to me. And they taste like spicy little pieces of cheese heaven.

"Why aren't you finishing, Zayd?" Mama frowns.

"My stomach hurts a little." Oops. Now Mama is going to want me to write this down in that food journal. And my stomach doesn't *really* hurt. It just feels a little hungry for something other than spinach cake. Like a new basketball hoop. And making the gold team. And kids putting posters of me up on their walls one day. Some Cheetos wouldn't hurt either.

5

“Bye, Mama!” I jump out of the car and grab my lunch bag and violin. A teacher holds open the door to the school entrance by the gym for me, and I dash inside.

“No running!” he orders. I slow to a run-walk since I’m late for violin practice. The advanced orchestra meets in the mornings before school twice a week. My mom was super excited when Ms. Sterling invited me to join it. She doesn't even complain about having to drive me to school extra early.

As I pass the gym, I hear whistles blowing and peek inside. Adam, Blake, and a couple of other kids from the gold team are there, running up and down the court. I'm so surprised to see them that I stop in my tracks.

"Hey, Zayd!" Adam waves me in.

"What are you doing here?" I ask him. "Don't you guys have practice in the afternoon?"

"Yeah, but we got dropped off early. Mr. Lee says he's in here anyway, so we can use the

gym. As long as no one else signs up for it."

"You're so lucky."

"Wanna play?" Adam flicks me the ball, and I grab it. SMACK! My violin case hits the gym floor. I'm glad it's padded inside.

I pause for a moment, holding the ball. What should I do? Play basketball with my friend, or practice scales with Abigail and Ms. Sterling like I'm supposed to?

"Here." Adam holds up his hands, and I throw him the ball. And then I pick up my violin again and . . . shove it against the wall. I fling my backpack next to it and run onto the court.

Our gym has shiny floors that make that squeaky sound if your sneakers are new. But we hardly ever get to play basketball in it. During recess we go outside if it isn't raining. With so many kids crammed on the blacktop, there's barely any room for a game. When there's indoor recess, we have to stay in our classrooms and play board games or talk quietly. In gym class we do other stuff, like climbing ropes and playing pickleball. I thought pickleball was a joke. But it's a real sport, like squash and my grandpa's favorite: cricket. I don't understand why they name sports after gross foods and insects.

Right now we have the full court all to ourselves. We get to use two regulation-height hoops that aren't bent. And Adam found a good indoor ball with lots of grip.

We play three-on-three, and I make a

few slick dribble moves and a couple of long-range jump shots. Then we play a game of H-O-R-S-E, and I come in second.

"You're trying out for our team, right?" Adam says when the early bell rings. We walk back to where my stuff is piled on the ground. Like most of the boys in my class, Adam's a lot taller than me. Lately he sways from side to side when he walks, like some of the fifth graders do.

"I already did." I think back to the tryouts we had in the summer, when I played terribly. Adam and Blake went to the gold team, and I was placed in the D league.

"Yeah. But you choked."

I pause. What if I don't make the team *again*? I hadn't considered that before.

"Maybe," I finally say. I don't mention that I've been planning on it all along.

"If you just practice with us in the mornings you'll make it. You're good enough."

Adam thinks I belong on the gold team too! I hide a smile and act cool.

"Okay," I say. "Promise you won't tell my mom. She'll kill me if she finds out I'm skipping orchestra."

"I won't." Adam puts his hand up and gives me the peace sign. "Scout's honor."

"That's not the Scout sign. I was a Cub Scout," Blake says. "It's this." He throws up a fake gang sign.

"No, it's this." Adam punches Blake in the shoulder, and then they start wrestling in the hall.

I *really* want to be on their team.

I walk the long way around the school to my classroom. That way I avoid passing the music room and bumping into Ms. Sterling. But this was a million times better than practicing the violin. I'll figure out an excuse about why I can't come for the next few weeks. And then I'll practice violin extra hard after tryouts to make up for it. Promise.

6

I was destroying the other team in NBA 2K when my mom called me upstairs this afternoon.

"You can play video games with Jamal Mamoo later. I need you to do other things right now," she said.

"Mamoo's coming? Today?" Mama's younger brother Jamal Mamoo has a beard and a job and everything, but he doesn't act like a grown-up. When he comes over, he hangs out with me in the basement or plays outside, instead of sitting with the adults. He taught me my killer serve in Ping-Pong. He shows me the funniest videos ever on YouTube. And he has the wackiest laugh, which makes everyone around him crack up, even if they didn't hear the joke.

"He's having dinner with us. I need you to help Zara empty the dishwasher, sweep the kitchen, and practice violin," Mama said. "Are you practicing? I haven't heard you in a while."

"Yeah," I mumbled. I made a mental note: Practice violin today so that wouldn't be a lie.

I did everything she asked without any complaining, thinking about all the fun I'd have later. Except now that mamoo is finally here, everyone else is hogging him.

Zara is perched on the armrest of Jamal Mamoo's chair, asking a million questions.

"Oh my God! Where are you going to meet her? What's her name? Where's she from? Do you have a picture?" She barely stops to breathe.

"Relax, Zara." Mamoo laughs. "A friend of Ammi's suggested I meet her. And I agreed. That's all. Don't start planning the wedding."

I can't believe it. I cleaned my room for *this*? Jamal Mamoo of all people is talking about *marriage*? He's the guy who ignores everyone's questions about marriage. He always rolls his eyes when Naano talks about finding him a "nice girl from good family." Or he says things like, "I'll get hitched when Zayd does."

"You sound like the cheesy younger brother

from *Dil Nahi Chahta*," I finally blurt out when I can't take it anymore. That guy is always meeting girls who never like him. It isn't a compliment.

"What did you say?" Jamal Mamoo gets up and stands over me. His crosses his arms and bugs out his eyes.

"Nothing," I say, shrinking into the couch.

"Really? Because I heard you." Jamal Mamoo tackles me and starts to tickle me.

"Stop! I'm going to pee!" I scream. I mean it. If he doesn't stop, I'm going to wet myself.

"Knock it off," Mama orders with a laugh. "I just steam cleaned."

Jamal Mamoo lets me go, and I'm panting and sweating now.

"I can't believe you're talking about marriage," I mumble.

"I can't believe how bony you are, Skeletor.

It hurts my fingers. Have you even hit sixty pounds yet, or what?"

Skeletor is mamoo's nickname for me because I'm skinny, and because he's a radiographer. I used to think that meant he worked at a radio station. But he actually takes pictures of people's insides with X-rays and other machines. He teases me and says that I look like the skeleton images he sees on the screen all day.

"Almost. I'm fifty-six pounds," I say.

"I wish he'd gain some weight," Mama says.

I hate it when people talk about me like I'm not even there.

"Some Cheetos might help," I suggest. Mama always says junk food makes you gain weight. But now she reads this nutrition blog that lists foods you should never buy your kids. And Cheetos were on it.

Jamal Mamoo lets out his wacky laugh.

"Your mom isn't buying you Cheetos!" he says. "But I'll make you a deal. You hit sixty pounds by the end of next month, and I'll get you an awesome prize."

"A new basketball hoop!" I shout.

"Uh. No. Think smaller."

"A signed Wall jersey?"

"Smaller. Like maybe a jumbo box of Cheetos." Jamal Mamoo laughs again while Mama starts to protest. "I'm kidding. I'll think about it. But you got to eat more and put on some pounds."

"Deal." We shake on it and then have a thumb war, which I lose like always. And then we play three games of NBA 2K, and I win two of them.

When I go up to my room at bedtime, I see the still-empty food journal sitting on my bedside table. I think about Jamal Mamoo's offer and flip it open to write in it for the very first time. If writing in this thing can do anything to help me put on some weight, I'm game.

DATE/TIME: 10/20, 8:47 p.m.

WHAT I ATE:

Almost all of the veggie burger Baba made (pretty good, but beef is better)

A slice of cheddar cheese, ketchup, and spicy barbecue sauce on the bun (whole wheat, not as good as sesame buns)

A handful of sweet potato fries (good, dipped in spicy barbecue sauce)

Spicy barbecue sauce

A few bites of salad (just for you, Mama!)

2 slices of the blueberry-peach pie Jamal Mamoo brought (now THAT'S what I'm talking about!)

HOW I FEEL: Super full, but a lot heavier already. I'm so getting that prize!

7

"Hey, Zayd!" Adam gets dropped off at school at the same time as me. A jolt of guilt hits me as I get out of my mom's car. She thinks I'm going to orchestra practice, even though I haven't been there in two weeks. But the feeling disappears as I follow Adam into the gym.

"My birthday's going to be at the trampoline place," Adam says. We peel off our jackets and pile our stuff by the door.

"My cousin had his party there. It was so fun."

"Did you do the basketball trampoline? You can jam the ball and everything."

"Yeah! It's awesome!" I say. "I did a three-sixty dunk and then fell on my face. But it didn't hurt."

"But you're always falling down," Adam reminds me.

"True."

Baba says I get knocked over easily because I'm so light. He also tells me I need to grow stronger and gain muscle. I've been eating as much as I can. I do push-ups and sit-ups and run sprints during basketball practice. What else am I supposed to do?

"Sorry I'm late. I turned off my alarm." Blake walks in wearing cool new sneakers with the Maryland flag design printed right on them. They are squeaking as he walks on the gym floor. I look down at my old shoes. They're dirty and worn out. But they still fit me, and there's no way I'm getting new ones until my feet grow. But I can't seem to make that happen any faster either.

"Where is everyone?" Adam looks at the clock. "Maybe Cody and Zane aren't coming today."

Adam acts like the coach of our morning practices, but no one seems to mind. He's always been someone that people listen to. Some might say bossy. But we've been best friends since first grade, and it's never bothered me.

"What should we do while we wait?" Adam asks. It's only been two weeks, but the extra practices are making a difference. I wonder if Coach Wheeler has noticed during my own team's practices.

"Let's do the halftime challenge like they do at Wizards games," Blake suggests. "See if you can make a layup, free throw, and three-pointer in sixty seconds."

"What does the winner get?" I ask.

"A signed ball or tickets to box seats or something."

"No, I mean right now," I say.

Blake searches through his pockets.

"How about a watermelon Jolly Rancher?"

"It's on."

Blake goes first while I keep time. He makes an easy layup. Then he's stuck at the free throw line forever.

“Come on, Blake!” Adam shouts.

“Time’s up!” I yell. Blake falls to the ground and lies there like he’s dead.

I go next. I miss the layup the first time and then get the next one in. I run to grab the ball, double back to the free throw line. The shot goes in with a satisfying

“Nice!” Adam is looking at his watch. “Fourteen seconds to go. You can do this!”

I race to the three-point line with the ball in my hands. I bounce it a couple of times and then release the ball.

“ZAYD!” I hear a voice that sounds familiar yell out my name from behind me.

I whip my head around. And then I freeze.

Standing there, in the doorway to the gym, is my *mother*. She's holding my violin case. Her face is set in stone. And I miss the shot by a mile.

8

"Hi, Mama." I walk over to her like there's nothing strange at all about her finding me hanging out in the gym. Maybe she'll think I only came in here *because* I forgot my violin and had nothing else to do before school. Yeah! That's it! I was only shooting hoops because I had *no other choice*.

"What are you doing here?" she asks.

"I, um, well, I forgot my violin. Right? So I came here to shoot around until school starts." I drop my head and kick the floor as I speak.

"Oh, I see. You forgot your violin."

She's falling for this? I look up in surprise.

"For TWO WHOLE WEEKS?" Mama explodes. "I went to look for you in the music room. And I saw Ms. Sterling. And guess what she said?"

I don't say anything. But I find a tiny hole near the tip of my shoe.

"Answer me. What do you think she said?" Mama presses.

"That she didn't like my idea. To get me a seat belt for the next concert?" I try to joke. I sneak a glance at Mama now. She's almost as purple as the scarf around her neck. And she isn't smiling.

"No, Zayd. Let me think. She said something about . . . what was it? Oh, yeah. How you told her you can't come to morning practice anymore because your parents CAN'T BRING YOU!"

I'm pretty sure I'm still breathing, but I don't move.

"Zayd! Are you listening? Look at me!"

I meet Mama's eyes. If they could shoot laser beams, I would be dust right now.

"Sorry, Mama," I mumble.

"That's it? That's all you have to say? I get ready at the crack of dawn to bring you here in the mornings. I use my hard-earned money to pay for your lessons. And you LIE to me and to your teacher and come in here to BOUNCE A BALL around?"

I nod my head. The way she puts it, it does sound like a bad idea.

"And how long were you planning to keep this up?"

"Um . . . I don't know. Maybe until tryouts?"

Mama shakes her head slowly. It looks like someone let all the air out of her. All of a sudden I feel like a basketball has whacked me in the stomach. I need to sit down.

"Mama, ever since I fell off the stage, Ms. Sterling's been acting weird. During class she's always telling me to—"

"Don't you dare," Mama cuts me off. "This isn't about her. You need to own this, Zayd." She looks around as the early bell rings.

Adam and Blake are on the other side of the gym, quietly dribbling and pretending not to listen. I'm pretty sure they can hear us.

"Sorry," I mutter again. I take the violin from my mother and go pick up my backpack and jacket.

"We'll discuss this later at home," Mama says. As Adam passes us, she gives him a stern stare. Mama usually hugs Adam whenever she sees him. But I guess he's an accomplice right now.

"Okay," I agree.

As she leaves, Adam gives me a sympathetic look. Blake hands me the watermelon Jolly Rancher. But I can't eat it right now. I didn't win the contest. And I feel like I lost a whole lot. I just don't know exactly what yet.

9

I'd be lying if I said I'm not a little scared to go home. I walk slowly from the bus stop to my house and ring the doorbell since I forgot my key. Phew. Zara opens the door.

"Hey," she says. She's still turned around, watching the TV in the other room.

"Where's Mama?"

"Store. I made kettle corn," Zara offers. She holds out a bowl of the sweet-and-salty popcorn.

"I'm not hungry." I didn't finish my lunch, but I can't eat right now. My stomach twists into knots every time I think about what happened this morning.

"Okay." Zara walks back to the family room and settles onto the sofa.

I head up to my room. The food journal is sitting on my desk, staring at me. I haven't touched it again since my first entry. I remember my mom's face at school and decide it's a good time to listen to her. So I open it up and write:

DATE/TIME: 10/26, 3:27 p.m.

WHAT I ATE:

Half a turkey sandwich (minus the crust)

17 goldfish crackers, cheddar flavor

6 bites of my apple

Watermelon Jolly Rancher

HOW I FEEL: Like someone is dribbling a ball on my insides.

Then I do my homework, lie on my bed, and look at an old issue of *Sports Illustrated Kids* that Blake gave me. It's got an amazing photo of John Wall making a fadeaway jumper.

"ZAYD!" I hear my father calling me. So I drag myself off the bed and go downstairs.

"Have a seat," my dad says, pointing to the dining table. Mama is back and already sitting there. We never use the dining table except for parties, making posters for school projects, and family meetings. I feel my heart pounding in my throat.

I decide to apologize before he gets going. "Baba, I . . ."

"Hold on." Baba stops me as Zara walks into the room. She's carrying a book and wearing headphones. And she's pretending that she only happened to come into the room we never use. But we all know she's spying.

"Zara, can you excuse us, please?"

"Yeah, sure," Zara says. She gives me a look and mouths "You're dead!" on her way out.

Baba frowns, gives me a long stare, and then speaks.

"Your mother told me what happened. We're disappointed in you for lying to us. And to your teacher."

"Baba, I . . ." I start to apologize again.

"I'm not done. You committed to playing the violin. We paid to rent it. And we pay for you to be in the orchestra. It's a lot of money, time, and effort," Baba continues. Mama just nods her head.

I nod my head too.

"We know you like basketball. We've supported you. But now you lose it."

"What?" I gasp.

"You won't be playing any basketball for the next two weeks. And then we'll see after that."

"But I'm on a team!" I protest.

"You were in an orchestra, too, and you didn't worry about that. Your team will manage without you."

I feel my heart sink into my stomach as I realize tryouts are in less than two weeks.

"What about tryouts? I have to go to tryouts or I won't be able to move up to the gold team!" I know I should stop arguing, but I can't help it.

"You need to practice violin, to make up for the past two weeks. And you need to earn back our trust. Basketball is the least of your concerns right now."

I sit there, stunned.

"Do you understand me?" Baba continues. "No watching basketball either. Or reading about it. Or talking about it. I don't want to see that you are even thinking about basketball. Got it?"

I nod my head again and blink back tears. I can't believe I'm going to miss my chance to move out of the D league. Last time I lied to my parents, it wasn't on purpose. It kind of just happened. But right now I'm lying for real. Because I don't know how I'm not going to think about basketball. It's what I do more than anything else.

10

Even though Jamal Mamoo is meeting a girl to see if they might want to get married, we're all going. That means my family, Naano and Nana Abu, and mamoo have to drive all the way from Maryland to Virginia to this girl's house. And it means that I have to dress up nice to impress these people.

"That's what family's for," Baba declares when I grumble about wearing my button-down shirt with black pants. It's the same outfit I wear for orchestra concerts. And I don't need any reminders about that. My life has been all violin and no basketball for the past week.

"Try harder!" Mama orders while I shove my foot into one of the dress shoes that I found in a corner of the hall closet after searching everywhere. My heel won't go in all the way.

"When did you outgrow these?" she wonders aloud.

"I thought you wanted me to grow," I reply. Mama sighs. But Jamal Mamoo chuckles as I grab my sneakers.

"You wearing those, Skeletor? They're pretty beat up."

"I know. But they fit."

"How about that for your prize when you hit sixty pounds?" Jamal Mamoo suggests. "Some new kicks."

"Jordans?" I whisper so my parents don't hear me. I've wanted a pair of Air Jordans since forever, but my parents think they're way too expensive. Plus, I'm still being punished, and this conversation is technically about basketball.

"Yeah, sure," he says.

"Really?" I can't believe it.

"Come on, come on! We're going to be late." Baba rolls his eyes when he sees my shoes but doesn't say anything. We stumble out the door with arms full of gifts for the strangers: cake, flowers, a bunch of Pakistani sweets, and a fruit basket.

When we get there, an older auntie in a pink shalwar kameez and a scarf on her hair opens the door with a smile. A gray-haired uncle is standing behind her.

"Asalaamualaikum! Please, please, come in," they say.

We file into the house and take off our shoes. At that moment I see that one of my dressy black socks has a giant hole, and my big toe is completely sticking out. It must have ripped when I was shoving my foot into the tight shoe. I nudge Jamal Mamoo, and we both start to giggle.

"Shhhh!" Mama scolds as we make our way to a formal living room. There are sofas with carved wooden arms along the walls. Nana Abu settles into one of the sofas and smiles at everyone. But Naano looks like she is sitting on a pile of rocks and keeps squirming. I try to hide my naked toe under my other foot.

After a while, the auntie serves us drinks on a tray. I take a little napkin and manage not to spill as I lift up a soda, ignoring Mama's raised eyebrow. Of course soda is on the list of junk foods never to let your kids have.

And then the girl walks into the room. I feel bad for her because we all stare at her like she's an alien wearing a blue shalwar kameez. But she acts like she doesn't notice and smiles at all of us. She says salaam and "it's nice to meet you" in perfect Urdu. Then she takes a seat near Naano, who I can tell likes her already.

"This is Nadia," her mother says proudly.

I sneak a peek at Jamal Mamoo, who is

sitting next to me. He's turning red and acting like he's trying to look and *not* look at Nadia at the same time.

"It's nice to meet you, Nadia," Mama says. And then there's nothing but awkward silence.

"Nadia is finishing up nursing school," her father finally says after clearing his throat.

"Jamal is a radiographer." Nana Abu smiles. "That's nice, mashallah. They are both in the health field."

And then everyone is quiet again.

I give Jamal Mamoo a little nudge with my elbow. It means, "Dude, say something." But my loud, funny uncle has turned into this silent, sweaty, nervous guy. Next I try to poke mamoo with my big toe—the one that's sticking out. But he doesn't even crack a smile. In Naano's drama, the main character is always charming and funny when he meets girls. But mamoo is the total opposite.

"So, Nadia . . . um . . . auntie," I finally pipe up. "Do you like sports?"

"I do, Zayd," she says brightly. I'm surprised she knows my name. "Football and basketball most. What about you?"

"Yeah. Basketball most. Are you a Wizards fan?" I hold my breath. She could be the perfect wife. For Jamal Mamoo, I mean.

"I'm from Chicago. Bulls all the way."

"Oh." My hope fizzles.

But Jamal Mamoo takes my lead. "Cubs or White Sox?"

"Cubbies all the way!" she says.

As the two of them start talking about stadiums and good restaurants, the rest of us slowly leave the room. Zara and I end up watching a cartoon movie in the den. The grown-ups chat in the dining room. Naano is putting on a show and is telling her favorite jokes. I hear laughing and the sound of teacups clinking. And I remember the Jordans and help myself to an extra-big slice of cake from the table.

As we leave, Jamal Mamoo stops me in the hall and gives me a friendly shove.

"Hey, Skeletor. Thanks for jumping in. That was a good call."

"No problem," I say. "I got you."

As I shove mamoo back, I decide that Baba was right about that whole "that's what family's for" thing after all.

11

Ever since I've been grounded, Zara's been rubbing it in my face.

"Can you believe Wall and Beal both got double-doubles last night? Wall scored twenty-three points in the second half."

I make a face at her over my cereal.

"Oh, yeah. You couldn't watch the game." She fakes a sad face. "Want to shoot around?"

Now I stick my tongue out, covered in mushed oat flakes and milk.

"Oh, man, that's right. You can't. How about we play some 2K?"

"YOU'RE NOT FUNNY, ZARA!" I shout, glad when little drops of cereal milk spray out of my mouth in her direction.

"Zayd! Don't yell at your sister," Mama says as she walks into the kitchen. "I need you to practice violin, then get ready. I'm dropping you guys off at Naano's."

"Why?" I ask.

"Baba and I are going to the mosque to plan the fund-raiser. Would you rather come? I don't think kids will be there."

"I want to go to Naano's," I say. I drag myself to the living room and pick up my violin. I wonder if everyone else in the house is sick of hearing me play "Song for Christine" over and over. I imagine my parents wearing earplugs and secretly wishing I was playing basketball instead. It makes me feel a little better about my punishment. I play as loudly as I can.

When we arrive at my grandparents' house, Naano opens the door in her fuzzy slippers.

"Zayd. My skinny mouse. Let's eat something. What you want? Zara, come."

"I'm good, Naano. I promise I already ate," I say as I walk into the family room, where the TV is on, like usual. But instead of dramas or Pakistani news or cricket, Nana Abu is watching a game I've never seen before.

"What is this, Nana Abu?" I ask.

"Kabaddi," he says.

"Ka-buddy?"

"No, kabaddi," he repeats.

"That's what I said. What are they doing?"

"I played this game when I was a boy. This is the world cup." Nana Abu sounds proud. But he doesn't explain how the game works, so I try to figure it out.

The teams are on opposite sides of a court. One person from each team tries to tag a player on the other team. And even though it sounds like a joke, the defenders all *hold hands* and hop around. And then the tagger, who the announcer is calling a "raider," starts to bob and weave, like a boxer. Sometimes the chain breaks and the other team grabs him and throws him to the ground. It looks confusing, like tag and wrestling and ring-around-the-rosie at the same time.

"When I was a boy, in my village, we would wear nothing but our chaddis and grease our bodies with oil so the other team couldn't

grab us," Nana Abu explains with a gleam in his eye.

"Were you on a team?" I ask.

"Not a team like yours," he says. "We made our own teams. But, oh, it was so much fun."

"I can't play on my team anymore," I say. "My parents won't let me."

"That's because he lied," Zara volunteers.

"Why you tell lie?" Naano asks. "Serves you right."

But Nana Abu gives me a gentle smile.

"I'll teach you a new game," he says.

"Ka-buddy?" I ask, worried. The last thing I need to do is wrestle my slicked-up grandfather wearing nothing but giant underwear.

"No. This game is called carom. Come with me."

Nana Abu shuffles over to the closet and pulls out a large square wooden board with pockets in the corners. He finds a box with disk pieces in it. Zara and I help him lay the board flat on a small side table and sprinkle powder on it. The disks slide around on the smooth board like an air hockey table, without the air.

Nana Abu arranges the pieces in the middle of the board. He points to a bigger disk. "This is the striker. This is the queen," he says, motioning to a red piece. "That goes in last."

"It's so cute," Zara says. "Like a tiny pool table."

She's right. Except instead of a pool stick, in carom you use your fingers to flick the striker toward the pieces you want to get into the pockets.

We spend the afternoon challenging Nana Abu and losing to him each time. But I get the hang of it faster than Zara and easily beat her.

"I can't get the pieces in!" Zara whines. She isn't used to not being the best at something.

I, on the other hand, do know what that's like. So for the next hour it feels great to cream her at carom, my new second-favorite game. And I make sure to rub it in, just a little. Okay, a lot.

12

"Great job, Zayd." Ms. Sterling doesn't hide the surprise in her voice. "I can tell you've been practicing."

"Thanks," I mutter. I have to admit that I can tell I sound better too. But it doesn't make me like playing the violin any more. I know my friends are still playing basketball on the other side of the school. And that's where I want to be.

"You know, Zayd," Ms. Sterling continues, as if she is reading my mind. "Many famous athletes are musicians. It's a great way to relax."

"Really?" I ask. "Like who?"

"Well, Shaquille O'Neal recorded music for starters," she says.

"I guess so." I pack up my instrument and don't tell her Shaquille O'Neal recorded *rap* music. I'd love to do that too.

Ms. Sterling makes me think of basketball again, and for a moment I hope we can play at recess. Until I remember my punishment. No basketball for a few more days. Plus it was raining this morning, so we'll probably be stuck inside anyway. It's been raining a lot this week, and we've had indoor recess every day. It's making everyone grumpy.

We've been playing cards in our classroom since we can't go outside. Adam taught Blake and me how to play Egyptian War. It's like regular War, except you throw down your cards really fast, you can play with more than one other person, and you have to slap the cards whenever there are two of the same. If you slap the cards first, you get the whole pile. Whoever gets all the cards wins.

"You didn't shuffle," Adam complains. It's recess, and we're in the classroom with our cards.

"I did too. You saw me," I argue.

"You have all the jacks. No fair."

We throw our cards down so fast it's almost a blur. But then I spot two sevens.

THWACK!

Adam's hand slaps the table, and my hand hits the top of his.

"Ha! Got it!" He grins.

We start throwing cards down again, and this time I see two queens.

THWACK!

I get there first, but Blake tries to slide his hand underneath and jabs me with his fingernail.

"OW!" I howl.

"SHHH. Boys, keep it down," Mrs. Neal orders.

"Nasty! Cut your nails! They're disgusting," I grumble.

Blake inspects his nails.

"Doesn't bother me." He shrugs.

"Yeah, but remember when half of Cody's nail ripped off during basketball practice?" Adam warns him. "You should cut them."

"Yeah," I agree. I rub my hand and make sure he didn't draw blood.

"When can you play with us again?" Adam asks me. "Isn't your punishment over?"

"Almost," I say. "But I'm back in orchestra in the mornings anyway."

"Wait. You're still coming to tryouts, though, right?" Adam looks worried.

"I'm still grounded then."

"No way! That sucks." Adam frowns.

"I would die if I couldn't play basketball for so long," Blake adds.

"Yeah."

"Maybe you can get Coach to let you try out later." Adam is trying to encourage me, like usual.

"I don't know. Coach might be mad at me already." Mama e-mailed Coach Wheeler to say I wasn't going to be at practice or games for the two weeks I'm being grounded. I wonder what will happen when I go back. Maybe he'll make me sit on the bench.

"Well, he can't kick you out of the D league," Blake chimes in. "Can he?"

"Dude, you're not helping." Adam punches Blake in the shoulder. "You'll figure it out, Zayd, don't worry."

I can't help but worry, and I think about missing tryouts all day. Mrs. Carson says I'm "distracted" during science, when she calls on me and I'm not paying attention. But while she goes on and on about genetics and earlobes, my stomach starts to hurt. This time it's really hurting, like someone is wringing out my insides like a sponge.

I raise my hand.

"Can I go to the nurse?" I ask.

13

"Zayd, I haven't seen you in a while," Mrs. Diallo says when I walk into the small health room by the office. "What's the matter?"

"My stomach hurts. Can I lie down?"

"Sure, honey. Do you need me to call your mom?"

"Okay," I moan. I crawl onto the little cot by the door. It smells like the tub of Clorox wipes sitting on the table next to it.

"Mrs. Saleem?" I hear Mrs. Diallo speaking into the phone. "I have Zayd at the nurse's station. He's complaining of stomach pain. Oh, let me ask."

Mrs. Diallo turns to me. "Zayd? Mom is asking if you need to use the bathroom?"

"Um. No," I say. I feel my face grow hot. Isn't that *personal*?

"He says no. Oh, I see. Okay. I'll let him know. Thanks," Mrs. Diallo continues into the phone.

"Is she coming?" I ask.

"She says someone will come pick you up."

"Okay." I close my eyes, trying to shut the pain out. I play the song we were practicing in violin in my head and lie there, curled up in a ball.

The next thing I know, I feel a gentle shaking. I open my eyes to see Jamal Mamoo standing over me in light blue scrubs. I must have fallen asleep.

"Salaams, Skeletor," he says.

"Salaams," I say, rubbing my eyes.

"How you feeling?"

"Better. My . . ." I start to say that my stomach isn't hurting anymore. But Jamal Mamoo shakes his head and winks at me. So I stop talking.

"Where do I sign him out?" he turns and asks Mrs. Diallo in his most charming voice.

"Next door, in the main office. Feel better, Zayd," she says.

"Thanks." I try to sound more miserable than I feel.

We walk out to the parking lot after I go collect my backpack, lunch bag, and violin from my cubby. I feel guilty because everyone looks sorry for me, and I'm totally fine. My stomach doesn't hurt a bit. It's like nothing ever happened. Plus it's finally stopped raining, and the sun is starting to peek out.

"But, Mamoo, I'm okay now," I whisper, even though we've left the building and are almost at his car. "I can go back to class."

"I had to drive all the way out here. And if I'm missing work, you're skipping the rest of the day. Deal?"

"Deal," I agree. "Where are we going?"

"Hungry?" he asks.

"Kind of."

"Let's get some chicken."

14

We pull up in front of a place called Crisp & Juicy.

"Don't tell Naano, but this is the best chicken in town. You like plantains and yucca?" Mamoo doesn't wait for me to answer and orders a family platter, for the two of us.

"So, what's going on with you?" he asks

after he carries the tray to a table in the corner. Mamoo tears the chicken apart and puts a huge piece in front of me. "This should help put some meat on you. Try this sauce."

I take a bite of the chicken. Like the restaurant's name, it's crisp and juicy, and delicious.

"What happened to you today? Did you have a test? Someone mean to you?"

"No."

"Well, then, what's going on with you?"

"Nothing."

"What were you thinking about when your stomach started hurting?"

"Tryouts. I've been dying to be on the gold team. And now I'm going to miss my chance since I can't go. I haven't played any basketball for nine days, when I should have been practicing extra hard. I've missed all the

Wizards games on TV. And I can't even play 2K." Everything pours out.

"Oh, I see." Jamal Mamoo's forehead wrinkles. "Do you have a cough?"

"No."

"Body aches?"

"No."

"Do you drool when you sleep?"

"Maybe a little."

"I think I know what you are suffering from."

"What?" I ask.

"*Agonia hoopidynia*. Sounds like a bad case." Jamal Mamoo shakes his head sadly.

"WHAT?"

"*Hoopidynia*. Haven't you heard of it?"

"Oh my God. Is it serious?"

"I think you'll survive. But you'll need treatment."

"Does it hurt?" I feel my stomach tighten again.

"As bad as when I destroy you in one on one."

I finally realize he's teasing me. HOOP-idynia. Corny.

"Very funny, Mamoo. You freaked me out!"

Mamoo grins, then gets serious.

"Listen, Zayd. You need to stand up for yourself. Tell your parents how much these tryouts and this team mean to you. Maybe they'll understand why you did such a boneheaded thing."

"But Mama wants me to play violin more than basketball. I've been playing so much violin it's ridiculous. I want to quit and focus on basketball."

I've never said that before, but it's true.

"I get it. You need to make them understand what *you* want. For yourself."

"Have you ever tried to change my mom's mind about anything?" I ask.

"Good point." Mamoo smiles. "Just be strong."

I chew for a minute and think about what he said. Then I say what else is on my mind.

"What about you? *You're* not standing up for yourself."

"Excuse me?" Mamoo raises his eyebrows.

"You're letting everyone make you get married."

Mamoo laughs so loudly the people at the other tables all look at us. One lady even starts to giggle even though she doesn't know why.

"Nice try, Skeletor. It's not that. I'm just realizing that it might finally be the right time to find someone. You don't want me to be alone forever, do you?"

"I guess not."

"Look, there's a difference between letting your family guide you and letting them stop you from following your true passion. Get it?"

I suddenly think about the poor guy in *Dil Nahi Chahta* trying to make movies while his parents freak out about medical school. I nod my head. And I decide that I hope he gets to make his movies, even if they look like ones I'd never want to watch.

"I have faith you can convince your parents," mamoo says as he pulls a leg off the chicken and drops it on my plate. "And that you'll eat more chicken. I can't finish this platter by myself."

15

At night, before bed, I take a deep breath and march into the family room. Mama and Baba are sitting on the sofa with their laptops. I make sure Mama isn't paying bills, since that makes her cranky. She's online, looking at someone's wedding photos. That's a good sign.

"Mama? Baba?" I say.

"Hey, hon. What's up?" Mama's still looking at the screen. I would get in trouble for doing that.

"You tell me that I should always be honest with you, right?" I start.

"Of course," Mama says. She's giving me her full attention now. I imagine serious violin music playing in the background and try to push it out of my head.

"I know I should have told you I was skipping violin. But the honest truth is, I don't want to play it anymore."

"What do you mean?" Mama starts to shake her head. "You've been playing for more than a year now. And you're good at it!"

"But I don't like it. I don't like practicing it. I don't like my lessons. I don't like being in the orchestra. I don't even like the way the violin *sounds*."

"That's absurd," Mama snorts. "How can you not like the way a violin sounds? It's beautiful."

"Maybe to you," I continue. "But I like hip-hop."

Mama looks crushed.

"But you have so much potential," she says. "You'll learn to appreciate it."

"I don't want to. I want to play basketball. And be on the gold team. And I skipped violin because I wanted to have a better chance at tryouts."

"But, Zayd, you're so . . ." Baba stops himself and looks a little embarrassed.

I wait for him to finish.

"The other kids have a real size advantage over you. Don't you think it makes more sense for you to . . . um . . . maybe focus on a different sport?"

"Like what?"

"Like tennis. Or swimming. You were always a good swimmer."

"I'm good at basketball, too. I've gotten a lot better than I was. At least I *was* getting better. Before you made me stop."

Mama and Baba look at each other.

"Plus all my friends play basketball," I add.

"Well, if all your friends—" Baba starts.

"I promise I would *not* jump off a cliff," I interrupt.

Baba smiles.

"I was going to say that if all your friends play, I can see why you want to also. But don't jump off a cliff, either."

"Can I please, PLEASE go to tryouts this weekend? My two weeks are almost up. I can make up the extra days later? Please?"

"We appreciate you being honest with us,"

Mama says. "Let your dad and me talk about it."

I start to feel lighter.

"But you know that it's good to stick with something you start," she adds. "And you've already invested time and energy learning to play the violin."

"Zara got to quit tap dance," I mumble. "And softball. And kung fu."

"Okay, Zayd. It's not a competition with Zara." Mama picks up her laptop again, but her eyes are smiling. "Besides, playing the violin is different. It helps develop your brain. We just want to help you grow."

I don't say that it won't help me grow heavier or taller. And that's the only kind of growing I'm really interested in right now.

"Just think seriously about this decision, and we will too," Mama says. "Okay?"

"Okay, I will."

Even though she still needs to think about it, I don't. I should have told them what I felt weeks ago. Ever since the day I fell off that stage I knew it was meant to be my grand finale. Like mamoo said, I need to follow my true passion.

16

"Gentlemen, are we looking up information for our research projects or goofing around?"

Mrs. Griffin is glaring at us over her reading glasses from the checkout desk in the media center.

"Looking up information," Adam says, as

he pokes me under the table. We're sitting at the computers to do research for our role-models project.

"Check this out!" Adam clicks on a YouTube video called "Kevin Durant's Greatest Moments." There are three guys in regular clothes talking about Durant and imitating his signature moves on a court. And they name each one something goofy like the Matrix.

"He's amazing," Adam sighs. "And you know . . ."

"I *know.* Your cousin went to high school with him at Montrose Christian. You told me a thousand times."

"You're just jealous."

"It wasn't *you,* was it?"

"Still. My cousin knows him. And I know my cousin. So it's like I know him."

"BOYS!" Mrs. Griffin sneaks up behind us,

and we both jump. "That does *not* look like research!"

"Yes it is." Adam turns to a page in his notebook and points to the title. "It's research, promise. Look. I picked Kevin Durant as my role model."

Mrs. Griffin lets out a big sigh. "A football player? That's the best you could come up with?"

"Basketball. And he *is* the best," Adam argues. "He's tall *and* he can shoot."

"Well, I hope you can find other reasons why he is a true role model. What about you, Zayd? Who do you have?"

"John Wall."

"Let me guess, another athlete?"

"Not just another athlete. He's MVP of the Wizards. He leads the league in assists. And he—"

"Okay, okay." Mrs. Griffin frowns. "I get the idea. But you need to find at least two reasons to admire these individuals outside of sports."

Adam and I look at each other. Mrs. Griffin is taking all the fun out of this project.

"And I expect you to use the Internet to look up articles, boys. No more videos."

"Okay," we both say.

I spend the next half hour trying to find out other stuff about John Wall besides his shooting average. And I'm surprised how much there is.

"John Wall's awesome," I say.

"Not as awesome as KD," Adam argues.

"I'm not talking about basketball. He won a Community Assist Award for doing all this cool stuff."

"Like what?"

"Helping homeless kids, and building

playgrounds and things." I point to the article on the screen. "And I touched him," I add.

"I know. You told me a thousand times."

Adam is just getting back at me for not acting impressed enough about Durant and his cousin. But I really did touch John Wall. It was when Jamal Mamoo took me to a Wizards game last year for my birthday, up in the highest section of the arena. Right before halftime we went down to the spot where the players pass by to go to the locker room.

I got to high-five most of the team, and even though I missed John Wall, I touched his arm as he walked by. His sweat absorbed into my skin. I told Mamoo I was never going to wash that hand again. He made me wash it ten minutes later when he bought me a hot dog. But it was still awesome. I *touched* John Wall!

Adam checks to make sure Mrs. Griffin

isn't looking and clicks on a website called Land of Basketball, where you can compare stats of players side by side.

"KD is better than Wall. No comparison. And he helps kids too," he gloats. "Look."

Durant has beaten Wall in every single category except for steals and assists.

I just shrug since I can't argue with the numbers. But Wall is still my favorite player. And he's going to be my role model, whether Mrs. Griffin likes it or not. Because you're supposed to learn something from a role model, right? And John Wall has taught me that sometimes you have to work extra hard to prove you're an all-star, even if others don't see it. And even if you're better than the team you're on. Plus, it's pretty cool that he likes to help people too.

17

"You need to man up," Zara sighs. "You can't fall down every time someone bumps into you."

"I'm not trying to," I grumble.

"Try to widen your stance a little, and press yourself into the ground," Jamal Mamoo suggests. "It'll make it harder for someone to knock you over."

"And you have to use your body more when you play," Zara adds. "Don't be afraid to be aggressive."

"I'm not afraid!" I want to shove her and show her how aggressive I can be. But I don't. Even though she's super annoying, Zara's trying to help for a change. Tryouts are in two days and I need all the practice I can get to make up for lost time. I'm just so happy that Mama and Baba agreed to let me try out. They said that they thought I had learned my lesson. And I don't even have to make up the last few days of my punishment.

"She's right, Zayd," Jamal Mamoo agrees. "You pass the ball too quickly when anyone presses you. You have to take it inside sometimes. Get into beast mode."

It's hard hearing everyone telling me what to do. I've been getting it from Coach, who was really tough on me when I went back to practice yesterday. Any time I missed a layup, he made me drop down and do ten extra push-ups. But I'm playing again, so I did it all without complaining.

"Here, try to get by me," Jamal Mamoo says. He passes me the ball.

I start to dribble, cut to my left, and then drive by him. He grabs me and picks me up, so I'm dangling in midair.

"No fair!" I yell while he laughs.

"Come in, you guys, and wash up for dinner!" Mama calls from the garage door.

I head inside and wash my hands, taking time to scrub all the black off, instead of just rinsing them.

"Zayd, come here for a minute." Mama pulls me into the family room before I go into the kitchen.

"I see how happy you are to be playing basketball again," she starts. "But I want you to remember why you were punished in the first place."

"I do."

"You know that you can always tell us what you want. Even if you think we won't like it, okay?"

"Okay."

"And I think it takes guts to say what you did about not wanting to play the violin the other night. Although I wish you would still play."

"Mama," I begin to protest. But Baba is standing behind her and signals for me to let her keep talking.

"I know, I know. I can't help that I do. But Mamoo reminded me how much I hated ballet when I was little and Naano made me take lessons."

"You did ballet?" I've never heard this before.

"For a little while. I used to cry about wearing those horribly itchy tights and that frilly pink tutu."

I imagine my mom in a tutu and fight back a smile.

"And I don't want to force you to do something you don't enjoy. Baba and I both want you to do what you love," Mama continues. "As long as you are always honest with us, Zayd. That's the most important thing. Understand?"

"Yeah."

"Okay, good. I'll tell Ms. Sterling that you're going to stop with the advanced orchestra. But will you still play during instrumental music, once a week? That way you can use the rental for the rest of the year."

"Sure," I say. That sounds fair enough. "I can do that."

"Great." Mama looks pleased.

"And, Mama, since we're being honest . . ."

"Yeah?"

"I wish you would cook normal food and let us eat junk again."

Baba gives me another signal that Mama can totally see this time: a double thumbs-up.

"Very funny, guys. That's not open for debate." Mama ruffles up my hair and gives me a hug. "Love you. Let's go eat."

"Love you too."

As we walk into the kitchen, it smells like we are at Naano's place instead of ours.

"Mmmm. What are we having?" Zara sniffs hard.

"Biryani," Naano says triumphantly. "And chapli kabob. I bring it."

"Yum." Baba grins.

"And for you, skinny mouse, mango lassi," Naano adds.

"But I don't like mango."

"Bakwas! Everyone likes mango," Naano

says before she realizes I'm kidding. Mangoes are my favorite fruit.

"*This* will make you fat and big," she says. We all know what she means. I've been eating so much lately. I'm still trying to get my new shoes from Mamoo. And I can use all the help I can get.

As I sip the sweet orange-colored milk shake, I look around the room. Nana Abu is piling a heap of biryani on his plate, and Mama is trying to squeeze some salad on the side. Baba is quizzing Zara on the periodic table of elements, and she is getting them all right. And Jamal Mamoo is buttering Naano up by telling her no future wife of his will ever cook as well as her.

After dinner I go upstairs and see my food journal by my bed. The other day Mama told me that she thinks my stomachaches happen when I'm worried about something, not because of an allergy or anything else. I think she's right. But they are happening less and less, which is good. The best part is she said I don't need to write in the journal anymore. But I flip it open anyway, just for fun, and enter in:

DATE/TIME: 11/9, 8:33 p.m.

WHAT I ATE:

A big pile of chicken biryani (Naano's masterpiece! Just the right amount of spicy)

1 1/2 chapli kabobs (if you pick out the tomatoes and onions, they are delicious)

Cucumber salad (chopped up cucumbers with salt and pepper on them that Naano took out for me, without adding yogurt to them. She's the best.)

A jumbo glass of mango lassi (which was amazing! Did I mention that Naano is the best?)

HOW I FEEL: Lucky

18

“Keanu! Pass!” I hold out my arms, and Keanu flings me the ball. I take a jumper and lose my balance. I’m falling. Again. But this time, as I hit the ground, I bounce and do a little somersault.

Keanu runs over and jumps on top of me,

and we bounce off the ground together. In a flash there's a huge pile of people on top of me.

"I can't breathe!" I shout. But I can't tell if it's because of the smelly socks in my face, or from laughing so hard.

"Watch this," Adam says after everyone rolls off me. He runs into the wall and does a half backflip into the middle of the trampoline.

No wonder Mama had to come inside and sign all these permission forms before Adam's party.

"Be careful, okay?" she warned. "You don't want to get hurt right before tryouts." So far three people have left the trampoline room limping. But there was no way I was going to sit out Adam's birthday party. And I survived without any twists or sprains.

"Time for cake, everyone," Mrs. Siegal announces.

We all crowd around Adam as he gets ready to blow out his candles. He looks around the room as we sing and then turns to me as he blows out his candles.

"You're going to do awesome at tryouts," he says. I squeeze by him to get a piece of cake. "You're going to make the team. I know it."

I don't ask if that's what he wished for. But I hope it is.

The next morning Mr. Siegal drives us to the middle school for tryouts. I try to ignore the mild churning in my stomach. I can't tell if it's the oatmeal Mama said would give me energy or my nerves. Maybe both.

When we walk into the gym, it's packed with kids.

"Why are there so many people here?" My voice is several pitches higher than usual. That has to be my nerves.

"This is fourth-, fifth-, and sixth-grade team tryouts. Don't worry," Adam says as we watch a kid who is almost six feet tall make an easy free throw.

Coach Wheeler blows the whistle and organizes us into groups. For the next hour he runs a bunch of drills. We start by running suicides back and forth across the gym. Then we do things like dribbling around cones and shooting from the free throw line and elbows. I make most of my shots and only flub my dribble once.

"You're playing like a boss," Adam says during water break. I hope he's right, because Coach Wheeler isn't giving away anything with his face.

Finally, we scrimmage. Somehow everything goes wrong. First, I botch a pass and turn the ball over. Then, on a fast break, I brick an easy layup. Worst of all I trip over my own feet while going for a steal and land on my face. OUCH!

I peel myself off the floor and avoid looking at Coach. I better do something to turn this around. And quick.

"Zayd!" Adam passes me the ball. I pump fake, and the defender takes the bait. I follow with a spin move and see the center coming to me. Before he gets to me, I step back into a fade-away jumper. Nothing but net! Adam gives me a high five. We would be awesome teammates.

On the next possession I steal the ball from a redheaded kid and lead my team down the court on a fast break. When I hit the free throw line, a defender jumps in my face. So I make a quick bounce pass to Adam, who finishes an easy layup. It's classic John Wall. I think he'd be proud.

I steal a look at Coach Wheeler and see a slight nod, as if he agrees with what I'm thinking. I'll take it. All I can do now is pray that I did enough to make the cut.

19

"I'm so full, but these noodles are so good," Zara says as she slurps chow mein off her plate.

I turn the disk in the middle of the table we're all seated around so I can reach what's left of the noodles. There is so much food spinning in front of me, it's dizzying. There's fried rice, chicken, shrimp, hot-and-sour soup and more.

We're at my grandparents' favorite Chinese restaurant, Good Fortune. It's also one of the only places Naano likes to go out to eat, besides IHOP. Most of the other places we've taken her to, she's picked at her food or said that it has "no taste." So we end up at Good Fortune a lot, which suits Zara and me fine, even if Mama complains about all the carbs, fat, sodium, and sugar. Tonight we're celebrating Nana Abu's seventy-third birthday.

Earlier I ran straight to Mama after I got home from school, and she was sitting in front of her computer concentrating on something.

"Did it come?" I asked.

"What, dear?"

"The e-mail! From Coach Wheeler! Did I make the team?"

"Hmmm. Let me check. I think it's right here. Oh, wait, can you hold on? I need to do something first."

"Mama! Really?" I felt like I was going to explode.

"It'll only take a second. I just need to stand up so I can . . . GIVE YOU A BIG HUG FOR MAKING THE TEAM!"

"I made it? For real?"

"For real!"

I let out a big whoop, and Mama wrapped her arms around me and squeezed me tight. Then Zara heard us and came running in, and soon we were all jumping and hugging like they do on TV sometimes. It felt great.

And now, at the restaurant with my

family around me, Jamal Mamoo tells us more news.

"I've been talking to Nadia for the past couple weeks, and she's cool."

"Oh my God! Does that mean you're getting engaged?" Zara asks.

"Not yet, but who knows. Right now I'm just getting to know a nice girl from a good family." He winks and looks at Naano when he says that last part.

"She is nice girl," she agrees. "And she has good family."

The waiter comes out with a little scoop of coconut ice cream and a lit candle in it, and we sing "Happy Birthday" to Nana Abu. Then Jamal Mamoo sings it again in a goofy mixture of English and Urdu. Nana Abu beams at us all and lets me blow out the candle.

"Thank you," he says as everyone hands

him gift bags filled with a new robe, slippers, and a book about Islamic Art. Zara and I printed out a card for him with photographs of us together, which he seems to like the best.

"And here's one for you," Jamal Mamoo says, putting a gift bag in my lap. "I'm proud of you for making the team, Skeletor," he adds. "And I'm sure you'll make the weight with all the food you just put away. Did you really eat all those noodles? Impressive, man."

I peek inside the bag and spot the logo on the box. It's a pair of Air Jordans! They are exactly the ones I wanted, black and red and perfect. I can't wait to wear them on the court and hear them squeaking. My heart beats faster as I think about showing up for the first practice with my new team.

"Thank you, Mamoo," I say. "Really. Thanks so much."

"You earned them. Now I need to see some serious balling from you."

We break into our fortune cookies next.

"Happiness comes from listening to your father," Baba pretends to read before he's even done pulling out the little paper. We all moan.

"Very funny, Baba!" Zara says.

"'You have an unusually magnetic personality.'" Naano grins as she reads hers. "Bakwas! But maybe it's good bakwas." We all laugh and agree that her fortune is legit.

"'Your smile brings happiness to everyone you meet.'" Nana Abu smiles. "Is that so?"

"Definitely!" Zara crunches her cookie. "Mine says, 'Next full moon brings you an enchanted evening.' I wonder what that will be?"

"Nothing at all, if I have anything to do with it!" Baba gives Zara an exaggerated warning look.

"I'll trade you yours for 'It is better to be the hammer than the nail,'" Jamal Mamoo offers. "What does *that* mean?"

"No thanks," Zara says. "I'm keeping mine. Let's hear yours, Zayd."

"Mama first," I say.

"'You love Chinese food,'" Mama laughs. "Okay, I confess. It's true! Sodium, carbs, and all. I love this stuff."

"And Zayd?" Baba prompts. "What does yours say?"

I swallow hard to try to clear the little lump that has formed in my throat.

"'You must power forward to achieve your dreams,'" I read in as deep a voice as I can.

"Right on!" Jamal Mamoo yells as everyone cheers for me. I take a little bow from my seat and look around as a warm feeling spreads throughout my insides. I wouldn't trade these people for anything. Okay, maybe just Zara. But only for a starting spot on the Wizards.

Looking for another great book?
Find it
IN THE MIDDLE.

Fun, fantastic books for kids
in the in-be**TWEEN** age.

IntheMiddleBooks.com

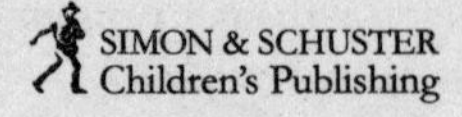

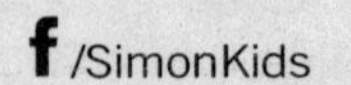

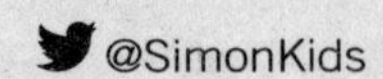

“Amina’s anxieties are entirely relatable, but it’s her sweet-hearted nature that makes her such a winning protagonist.”
—*Entertainment Weekly*

★“A universal story of self-acceptance and the acceptance of others.”
—*School Library Journal*, starred review

★“Written as beautifully as Amina’s voice surely is, this compassionate, timely novel is highly recommended.”
—*Booklist*, starred review

★“Amina’s middle school woes and the universal themes running through the book transcend culture, race, and religion.”
—*Kirkus Reviews*, starred review

PRINT AND EBOOK EDITIONS AVAILABLE

simonandschuster.com/kids

DATE DUE

The Library Store #47-0152